CASTLES

written by David Alderton
illustrated by Studio Boni/Galante,
Susanna Addarro *and* Lorenzo Pieri

CONTENTS

	page
Why Build a Castle?	5
A Stone Castle	6
A Day in a Castle	8
Attacking a Castle	10
Defending a Castle	12
A Knight	14
Close-up of a Castle	15
Knights in Peacetime	16
Building Castles	18
Castles Today	20
Castles Around the World	22
Palaces	24
Castle Timeline	26
Amazing Castle Facts	28
Glossary	29
Index	30

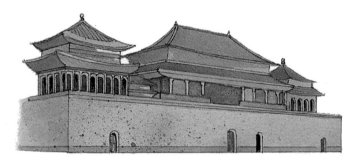

WHY BUILD A CASTLE?

As people started to live in one area, rather than moving from place to place, so they began to build homes. These settlements needed to be protected from attack. At first, people built simple earth walls round settlements to keep enemies out. These were the first castles.

An ancient hill fort
Hill forts, built in northern Europe around 3,000 years ago, had walls made of earth. The maze at the entrance was designed to deter enemies.

Motte and bailey castle
Earth was dug up to make a **moat**. This soil was then piled up to form a small hill, called a **motte**. This was surrounded by a fenced area of land, known as the **bailey**.

Stone castle
About 900 years ago, castles began to be built in stone. This was harder to destroy than wood, as wood can be burnt down easily. The **keep** was part of the main tower and was the safest part of the castle.

A STONE CASTLE

Many castles were designed to prevent attackers penetrating the castle walls. Round towers enabled enemies to be spotted more easily. Also, round towers were more difficult to knock down than square ones.

Shelter

When there was a risk of being attacked, local people would go into the castle.

The drawbridge

A drawbridge provided the way in and out of the castle, acting like a bridge. It was often fixed to chains. If danger threatened, the drawbridge could be pulled up, making it impossible to walk directly into the castle.

A DAY IN A CASTLE

Castles were mostly places where people lived and worked, rather than battle grounds. In peacetime, a castle would be a busy and exciting place to live in, with lots to do.

Religion
The day often began with prayers in the chapel.

Breakfast
There would have been bread and water for breakfast and perhaps some cold meat and fish as well. Food in those days had to be preserved by being dried, smoked or salted, as there were no fridges. Food supplies would be kept in the keep, where it was cool and dark.

Lessons
The children were taught to read and write by the priest. They learned a form of Latin. Girls were encouraged to sew, and the boys practised skills such as archery. Girls and boys might also play games like skittles and **stoolball**.

Hunting

Catching animals like boar or deer with dogs, and using hawks to hunt, were vital ways of providing food. Many kinds of birds were caught for eating. People also fished – eels and pike were favourite meals. There were more animals to catch in the countryside then, but it could be dangerous hunting some of them, such as wild boar.

Dinnertime

The household would eat meat and fish and drink wine in the great hall of the castle. People sat at long **banqueting** tables and were often entertained by minstrels, jugglers and other performers, between courses. At special feasts, as many as forty courses might be served.

Bedtime

The lord and lady slept in the **solar**. This room was built to catch the Sun and was the best bedroom in the castle. Most people slept in the great hall, where the fire would still be burning.

ATTACKING A CASTLE

An enemy army would have to plan an attack very carefully, trying to catch the occupants of the castle by surprise. The enemy army might try to climb over the walls or else knock down part of a wall. If this failed, the enemy might try to lay **siege** to the castle, trapping the occupants inside, without supplies of fresh food or water.

Crossbows and arrows
Archers with crossbows fired from behind a wooden screen, called a **mantlet**.

A siege could last for many months before the people in the castle surrendered. Special weapons were used to break through the defences of castles. Among the most deadly were gigantic catapults, called **trebuchets**. These could fire huge rocks as far as 100 metres into the castle. A large boulder could cause a lot of damage.

DEFENDING A CASTLE

If an attack was expected, there would be plenty of food and drink stored in the castle, in case of a siege. Once the army was sighted, the drawbridge would be raised, and the **portcullis** lowered, to make it hard for the enemy to enter here. Arrows could be fired through the slits, or **arrow loops**, in the castle walls. These openings gave the archers a good view, but were small, so that it was difficult for the enemy to fire back through them.

Cauldron
This was used to pour boiling liquids on people below.

Parts of the battlements stuck out. This meant that heavy stones could be dropped through the spaces here, which became known as **murder holes**.

Archery

Archers could use two types of bow. There was the longbow, made from yew wood, which was springy. The arrows, tipped with steel, were made of hard ash wood. Crossbows did not require as much strength to use. They fired shorter arrows but could be just as deadly.

A KNIGHT

There were different types of soldiers in an army. The knights rode horses into battles, and commanded men. Knights were protected by heavy armour and rode strong, powerful horses.

Helmet
A movable visor helped to protect the knight's face.

Sword
Pointed swords were more efficient at thrusting through gaps in armour.

Mace
Ridges in the head of the mace, concentrated the force of the blow.

Battleaxe
This weapon was especially useful on horseback

Shield
A symbol on the shield would be used to identify each knight. The design of the symbol was part of a special system called **heraldry**. When a knight died, his symbol would be passed on to his eldest son.

CLOSE-UP OF A CASTLE

The design of the doors and windows of a castle were important. The doors and gates could be closed if an enemy army was approaching.

Wooden projections
Some castles had wooden planks, called **parapets,** which stuck out over the tops of the walls. This was so that boulders could be dropped down on attackers more easily.

Arrow loops
These were narrow so people could not climb through.

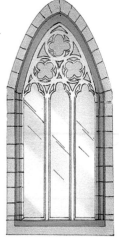

Castle turrets
Some kinds of turret jutted out from the sides of walls, and were called **machicolations**.

Great hall window
The lord and lady had a magnificent view of their land through this window. The design of the pointed arch at the top of the window is called Gothic.

The front door
The solid wooden door was kept firmly shut.

KNIGHTS IN PEACETIME

It could take ten years of study and work to become a knight. Boys from wealthy families training to be knights served as **pages** and then as **squires**. One of the squire's tasks was to clean the knight's armour. The knight taught the squire how to fight. Knights often took part in tournaments.

Knights charged at each other using long wooden poles, called lances. This was called jousting. For safety, the two knights were separated by a low wooden fence, called a tilt. If one knight was knocked off his horse, the fight would continue on the ground.

Some buildings were used for storing goods and also provided stabling for horses. Animals were kept in the castle, particularly if there was a risk of attack. Chickens often lived within the walls, pecking around on the ground, providing occupants with both fresh eggs and meat.

LIFE IN A MEDIEVAL CASTLE

Life in the castle was always busy, with people and goods entering through the **gatehouse**. Horses and carts were the main means of transport. Occasionally, oxen were used to pull the carts and also plough the fields outside the gates of the castle. Some castles had secret tunnels so that people could escape if the castle was surrounded by enemies. Many castles had stone toilets, built into the outer walls. There were various buildings made mainly of wood inside the walls of the castle.

A supply of fresh drinking water would be vital in the event of a siege. Without water, the occupants of the castle would soon have to surrender. Most castles were built with at least one underground spring inside their walls. This meant that it would be difficult for attackers to poison the water supply. There was little furniture in medieval castles, and no carpets. Dried rushes were often used to cover the bare floors. Sometimes, the walls were decorated with tapestries. There was no electricity or gas.

The most frightening part of the castle was the dungeon. It was dark and damp here. Prisoners could be kept in the dungeon for years, often spending most of their lives tied to the wall with chains. Prisoners sometimes carved on the stone walls to pass the time.

WHO'S WHO IN THE CASTLE

There were a wide variety of people in a castle. There were soldiers, who were needed in case the castle was attacked. A number of people with different jobs helped to maintain the castle, carrying out repairs when necessary. It was often possible to guess the kind of work which people did in the castle by the clothes they wore.

Soldier
Soldiers carried weapons such as bows and arrows and swords.

Jester
He could always be recognised by his brightly coloured costume with bells on his hat.

Minstrel
To entertain the household, minstrels sang and played instruments.

Serf
Serfs were manual labourers who helped with the upkeep of the castle and the surrounding land.

Bowman
He helped to protect the castle.

Running the castle needed a team of people. Money had to be collected in the form of taxes or rents to pay for the upkeep of the castle. Clerks had the task of keeping accounts, showing how much money was received and paid out, to ensure that the lord met his bills.

Constable
The constable checked that everything in the castle was in order. It was important to be aware of strangers who were visiting the castle, as there could be spies among them.

Marshall
The marshall organised the accommodation, especially when guests came to visit and stay.

Butler
Organising food was the butler's main responsibility

Steward
The steward's job was to make sure that the estate surrounding the castle was properly run.

17

BUILDING CASTLES

It usually took many years to build a castle. There were no powered machines to help with digging or moving materials. Just like today, people with specialised skills were needed to construct a castle. Over a thousand workers might be working on the building at one time.

The planning stage

The master mason would prepare the plans for the castle, to the lord's requirements. He would have had many years of training and experience.

Scaffolding

As the castle was built, wooden scaffolding was put up so that the builders could work on the walls. The scaffold poles were bound together with rope. Wooden planking was then laid on top. Ladders allowed the workers to move up and down easily.

Stonemason

Blocks of stone had to be carefully shaped by masons so that the stones would fit together properly.

Carpenter

Blacksmith

Working with iron and wood
Iron was used to make the portcullis, swords, armour and horseshoes. Like today, timber was used to make floors and furniture. It was also used as a structural frame to support large buildings. Wooden panelling was used to decorate some rooms.

CASTLES TODAY

The earliest castles that people built have vanished, but it is still possible to see their outlines from an aeroplane. Some castles have been preserved, but others have been left as ruins. These castles do not have roofs, because the timber used has rotted, leaving just stonework behind.

Chillon on Lake Geneva
This castle is more than 1,000 years old. It was once used as a prison. Many castles had dark dungeons, where prisoners were kept, often for many years.

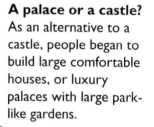

A palace or a castle?
As an alternative to a castle, people began to build large comfortable houses, or luxury palaces with large park-like gardens.

Windsor Castle
Windsor Castle is one of the homes of the British royal family. A fire swept through part of the castle, causing major damage in 1993.

Edinburgh Castle

The earliest remains of a castle on this site, in Scotland, can be traced back to AD 600. Edinburgh Castle was built on a steep-sided rock, which stands 130 metres above the surrounding ground. This rock is the remains of an ancient volcano. The castle overlooks the city of Edinburgh, which grew up under the protection of the castle. Even so, the English managed to capture this site several times during the Middle Ages, before it was taken back by the Scots.

CASTLES AROUND THE WORLD

Different types of castles have been built in many countries around the world. Although there are many different designs, castles were all built to defend an area of ground. Usually, castles were sited so it would be difficult for any attacking army to easily capture a castle. This meant that castles were sometimes built in odd shapes, especially if they needed to fit into a particular area. They were often built to protect communication routes, like roads and rivers.

Castles in different countries had characteristic design features. Those built in France, for example, had pointed roofs on their turrets, which look rather like witches' hats.

Krak des Chevaliers

This castle was built in Syria, in the Middle East, in the 12th century. Around the base, there were sloping mounds of soil, to prevent attackers being able to tunnel underneath. This castle still stands, although it has been damaged by earthquakes.

Ruins of Zimbabwe

There is an ancient ruined city, built in the 9th century, in the African country called Zimbabwe. Treasure – weapons and gold objects – have been found in the ruins.

The Tower of London

This fortress was built in 1087 in London, England by William the Conqueror. It is now home to the crown jewels. It is sometimes called 'The White Tower' because the keep's walls were painted with whitewash to make them look more impressive from a distance.

Rheinfels

One of the strongest castles ever built, Rheinfels stands on a steep rock above the River Rhine in Germany. Constructed in the 13th century it still stands today, having never been conquered in its entire history.

City of Azulchi

The fortress city of Azulchi was built in the 16th century by the warlords of Japan. The castle had a central tower seven storeys high and was covered with wall paintings and beautiful carvings.

PALACES

Castles were built to protect people, and so they were designed to have high walls and tiny windows. Palaces were built to be comfortable, luxurious homes, and to show how rich their owners were.

Hampton Court

This was built just outside London, England in the 16th century by Cardinal Wolsey who gave it to King Henry VIII. Like many palaces today, it is carefully restored and open to visitors. In the gardens there is a challenging maze made out of tall hedges.

The Alhambra

This 'Red Fortress' was built by the Arabs in Granada in Spain in the 14th century. It is made of pink bricks, and surrounded by beautifully landscaped shady courtyards and pools of water.

The Forbidden City

Walls and large gates surround the 'Forbidden City'. It was built in the 13th century in Beijing, China. Emperors lived within the Forbidden City walls with their families and many servants. Everyone else was excluded.

Chichen-itza

This is an ancient Mexican city, located in the Yucatan province, in Central America.

Chichen-itza was the centre of the Mayan empire. A temple built like a pyramid is shown here. There are many other buildings in the city, dating back to about AD 500. These include a courtyard made with a thousand columns, and an observatory tower, made specially to study the stars and planets.

Schönbrunn

This magnificent palace, built near Vienna, was the home of the Austrian emperors. It is nearly 300 years old, and has more than 1,400 rooms, including a theatre and a hall of mirrors.

Versailles

This splendid palace, near Paris, was originally built by the French ruler Louis XIII. His extravagant son, the 'Sun King' Louis XIV, spent a fortune making the palace and gardens bigger, better and more beautiful.

CASTLE TIMELINE

Castles are just one of many distinctive kinds of building where people have lived and worshipped throughout history. New ideas for creating different kinds of structures – pyramids, columns, arches and domes – have spread from different areas of the world. These architectural features create a legacy of landmarks, from different places and times, for us to visit.

1 Pyramid
Built in Egypt about 5,000 years ago.

2 Stonehenge
In Europe, people moved large stones to form structures about 4,000 years ago.

3 Greek column
The Greeks used columns to support roofs, about 2,500 years ago.

4 Roman arch
The Romans used intricate arches to support buildings, 2,000 years ago.

5 Hindu stupa
Buddhists built gold mounds, in Asia, 1,500 years ago.

6 Mosque
Built in the Middle East, around 1,450 years ago, using huge stone columns.

7 Aztec temple
Built by the Aztec civilisation in South America about 750 years ago.

8 Japanese castle
Built in Japan about 400 years ago, by nobles, called daimyos.

9 Taj Mahal
Built in India, about 300 years ago, as a tomb for an Indian empress.

10 Russian cathedral
Built in Russia about 300 years ago. Russian domes were specially shaped to stop snow piling up on them.

11 Empire State Building
Built in 1931 in New York, America. It has over a hundred storeys.

Since earliest times, castles, places of worship and important state buildings have provided people with a haven of safety.

AMAZING CASTLE FACTS

- **No windows** Glass was not often used in castle windows. Instead, the openings were covered by oiled linen, to protect against draughts, although this made the room rather dark.

- **Pigeons for food** Many castles kept pigeons, not as messengers but as a source of food.

- **The oldest castle** The oldest castle in the world was built in the Middle East. It stood twenty storeys high, and was constructed in AD100.

- **Beijing Palace** Moats around the Imperial Palace in Beijing, China, measure 49 metres in width – wider than many rivers.

- **A castle in two parts** Part of the castle of Burg Wildenstein was perched on a hilltop overlooking the River Danube in Germany. The other part of the castle was on a nearby hill. A tall tower with walkways linked them together.

- **Castle of horror** The Irish writer, Bram Stoker, first invented the legend of Count Dracula in 1897. He based the story on Vlad Dracula, a feared prince who once lived in a castle in Transylvania which is now part of Romania.

- **Monster hunting** The ruins of Urquhart Castle overlook Loch Ness in Scotland, and are supposedly one of the best places to see the famous monster which is rumoured to live in the Loch.

GLOSSARY

Arrow loops A hole in the walls of the castle, which allowed archers to fire their arrows on an attacking army.

Bailey The fenced area of land, below a motte, where people lived and worked.

Banquet An elaborate meal or feast, with lots of different courses, for lots of people.

Gatehouse The entry point to the castle, which was often heavily guarded.

Heraldry A system of creating and classifying knights, using symbols. It began in medieval times.

Keep The tower in the centre of a castle.

Machicolation Part of a battlement which stuck out over the castle walls, often with holes in the floor, so that heavy boulders and unpleasant liquids could be dropped down on to attackers.

Mantlet Wooden screen used to protect archers firing at the castle.

Moat Deep ditch surrounding some castles, which was usually full of water.

Motte Small hill made with earth dug from round a castle.

Murder hole A hole in the floor through which heavy objects were dropped.

Page A boy being trained for the medieval rank of a knight. While in training, the boy would be in the personal service of a knight.

Parapet A wall or rampart that protects the edge of a platform.

Portcullis A strong grating, usually made of iron, that protected the front door of a castle, preventing anyone from entering easily.

Siege A military blockade of a castle or city. The attacking army prevents any food, water or supplies coming into the castle, forcing the occupants to either surrender or starve.

Solar The biggest, best-lit bedroom in the castle, used by the lord and lady.

Squire A young man training to become a knight.

Stoolball A ball game, similar to cricket, which is characterised by underarm bowling.

Trebuchet Machine which fired boulders at the castle walls, to smash them down.

INDEX *(Entries in **bold** refer to an illustration)*

A   *pages*

Alhambra 24
archer 10, 12, 13
armour 14
Aztec temple 27
Azulchi 23

B

battlement 12-13
bedtime 9
blacksmith 19
boar 9
Burg Wildenstein 28
butler 17

C

carpenter 19
catapult 11
Chichen-itza 25
Chillon 20
constable 17
crossbow 13

D

design 15, 22
dinnertime 9
drawbridge 7, 12

E

Edinburgh Castle 21
Empire State Building 27

F

Forbidden City 24

G   *pages*

great hall 9, 15
Greek column 26

H

Hampton Court 24
helmet 14
Hindu stupa 26

J

Japanese castle 27

K

keep 5, 8
knight 14, 16
Krak des Chevaliers 22

L

lesson 8

M

mace 14
mantlet 10
marshall 17
master mason 18
maze 5, 24
moat 5
mosque 27
murder hole 13

P

page 16
palace 20, 24-25, 28
portcullis 12, 19
pyramid 26